BY DENNY J
3 Sentence
Fearful Fables
AF488079

Book Cover designed by Denny J

Design by Denny J

Intelectual Digital Art Ideas by Denny J

Written BY Denny J

Produced By Docslys Group LLC

This Book is Dedicated to
Mrs. Jackson
My One & Only

THE ROOM'S WALLS WERE PAINTED A DEEP RED WITH A BRIGHT GREEN STRIPE ALONG THE TOP. AS SOON AS I STEPPED INSIDE, I FELT A DEEP DREAD EMANATING FROM THE WALLS. SUDDENLY I HEARD A LOUD GROAN THAT SEEMED TO COME FROM BEHIND THE RED AND GREEN WALL - I KNEW SOMETHING EVIL WAS LURKING WITHIN.

THE OLD HOUSE CREAKED AS I STEPPED ONTO THE PURPLE FLOOR. IT SEEMED TO HAVE A LIFE OF ITS OWN, WITH THE BOARDS SHIFTING AND GROANING UNDERFOOT. AS I TOOK A STEP FORWARD, I HEARD A WHISPER IN MY EAR: "BEWARE THE PURPLE FLOOR, FOR IT WILL BE YOUR GRAVE!".

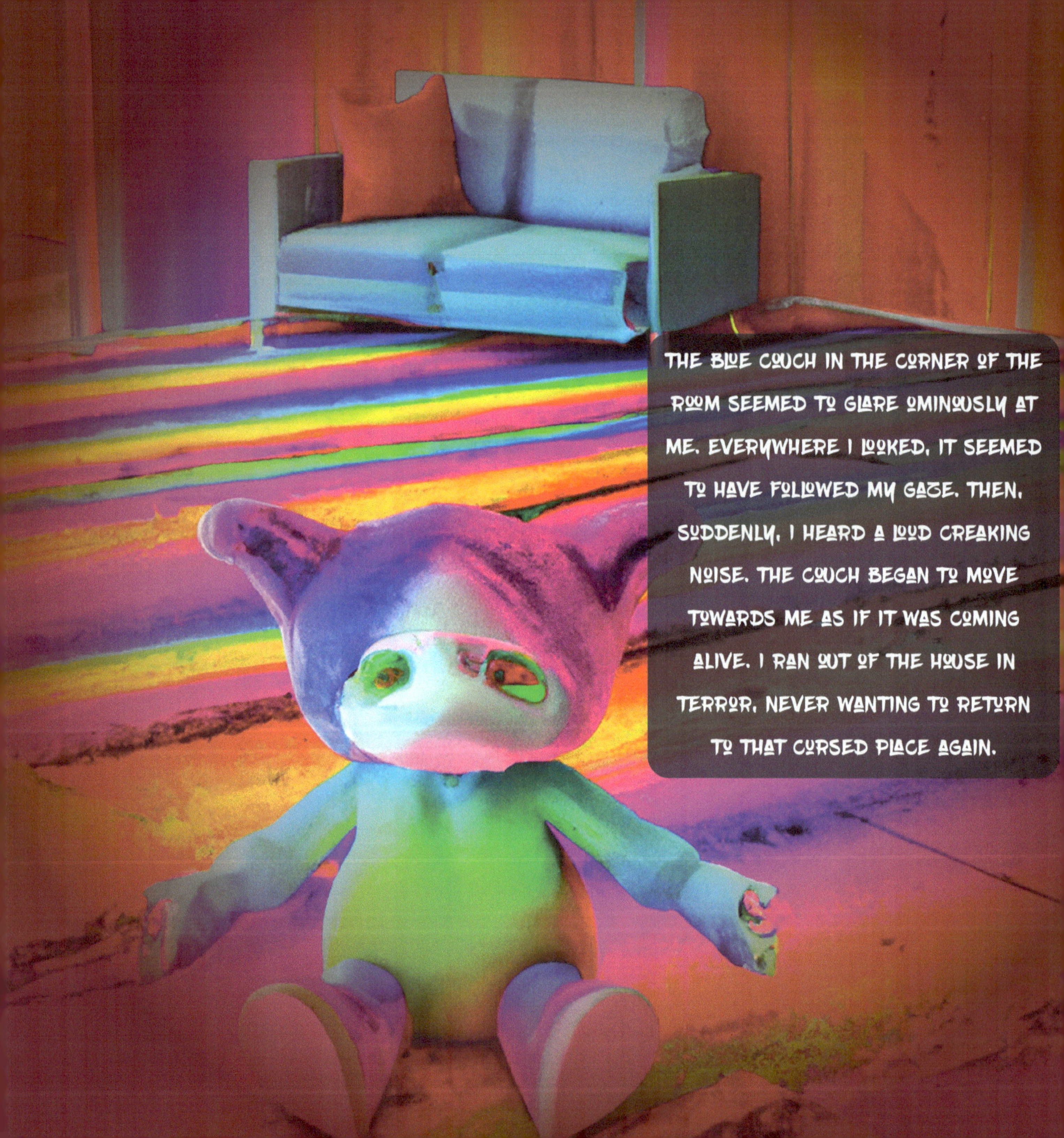
THE BLUE COUCH IN THE CORNER OF THE ROOM SEEMED TO GLARE OMINOUSLY AT ME. EVERYWHERE I LOOKED, IT SEEMED TO HAVE FOLLOWED MY GAZE. THEN, SUDDENLY, I HEARD A LOUD CREAKING NOISE. THE COUCH BEGAN TO MOVE TOWARDS ME AS IF IT WAS COMING ALIVE. I RAN OUT OF THE HOUSE IN TERROR, NEVER WANTING TO RETURN TO THAT CURSED PLACE AGAIN.

THE WALLS WERE LINED WITH STRANGE PICTURE FRAMES, EACH HOLDING AN EERIE PAINTING OF A DIFFERENT PERSON. EVERY TIME I LOOKED AWAY AND THEN BACK, THE FACES IN THE PHOTOGRAPHS HAD CHANGED TO LOOK JUST LIKE ME. I KNEW SOMETHING SINISTER WAS LURKING IN THE HOUSE, AND I HAD TO GET OUT BEFORE IT WAS TOO LATE.

THE PLANE RIDE SEEMED LONG AND TEDIOUS, BUT I WAS THANKFUL FOR THE EXTRA LEGROOM. AS I DRIFTED OFF TO SLEEP, THE RED EYES OF MY FELLOW PASSENGERS BEGAN TO GLOW IN THE DARK CABIN. I AWOKE TO A SCREAM, ONLY TO FIND OUT THAT NO ONE HAD BOARDED THE PLANE WITH US.

THE OLDER WOMAN SHUFFLED THROUGH THE DARK HALLWAY, HER PAPER CUTOUTS OF MONSTERS AND GHOSTS WHISPERING IN THE SHADOWS. AS SHE ROUNDED THE CORNER, PUSHDOWNS SEEMED TO TAKE ON A LIFE OF THEIR OWN, AND SHE FELT SOMETHING COLD BRUSH AGAINST HER ARM. SUDDENLY, HER PAPER MONSTERS WERE NO LONGER JUST CREATIONS OF HER IMAGINATION - THEY HAD BECOME REAL.

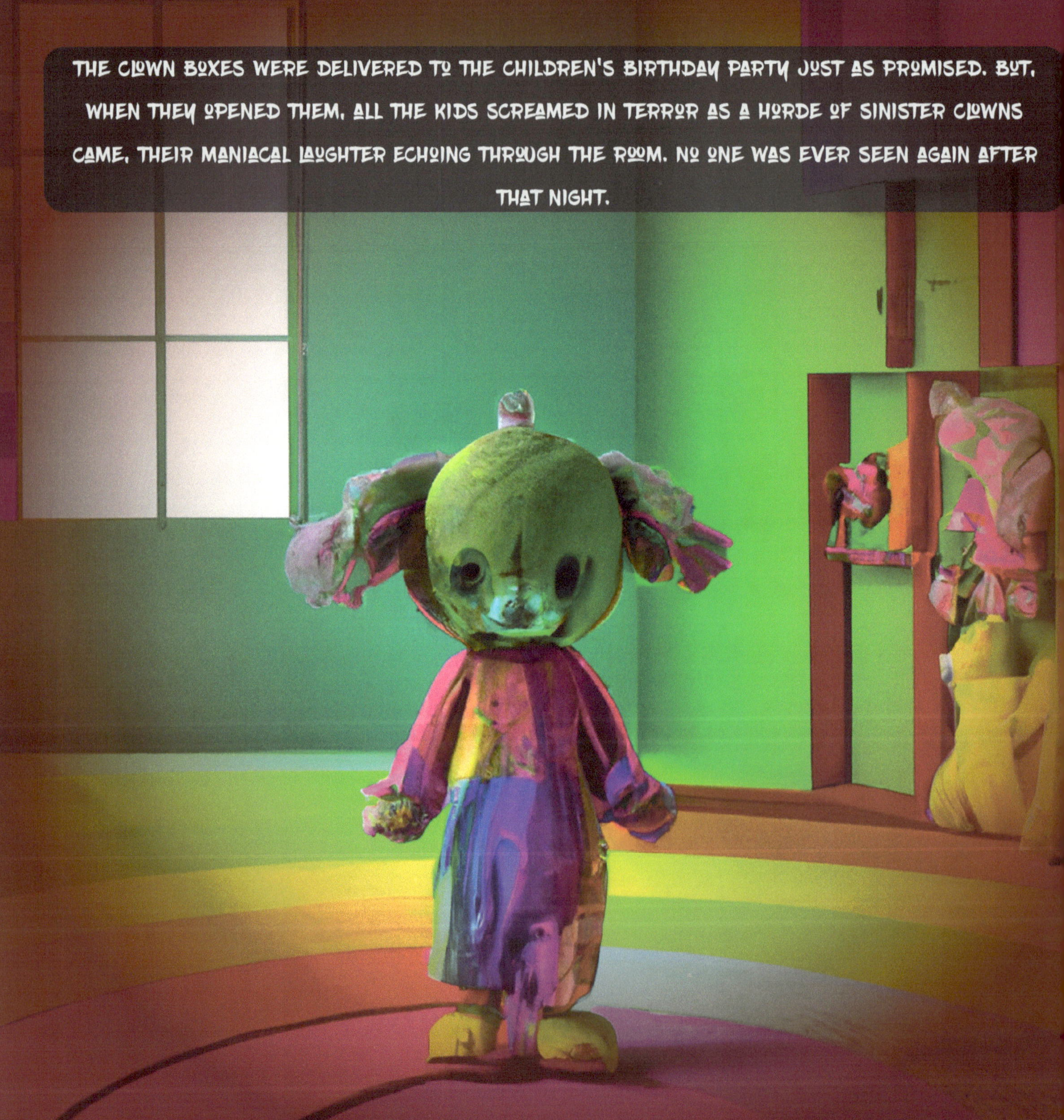
THE CLOWN BOXES WERE DELIVERED TO THE CHILDREN'S BIRTHDAY PARTY JUST AS PROMISED. BUT, WHEN THEY OPENED THEM, ALL THE KIDS SCREAMED IN TERROR AS A HORDE OF SINISTER CLOWNS CAME, THEIR MANIACAL LAUGHTER ECHOING THROUGH THE ROOM. NO ONE WAS EVER SEEN AGAIN AFTER THAT NIGHT.

THE TEDDY BEAR HAD BEEN LIVING IN THE CLOUD FOR AS LONG AS ANYONE COULD REMEMBER. EVERYONE HAD GROWN USED TO HIS PRESENCE IN THE SKY ABOVE THEM UNTIL, ONE DAY, SOMETHING STRANGE HAPPENED. SUDDENLY, TEDDY DESCENDED FROM THE CLOUDS AND BEGAN TO MARCH TOWARD THE NEAREST TOWN, HIS SINISTER LAUGHTER ECHOING AROUND THE LANDSCAPE.

MY DAUGHTER HAD BEEN OVEREATING CANDY LATELY, AND I WAS WORRIED. THEN, ONE NIGHT, I HEARD STRANGE NOISES COMING FROM HER BEDROOM. WHEN I WENT TO CHECK IT OUT, I SAW HER FACE TWISTED IN A HORRIFYING GRIMACE AS SHE STUFFED MORE CANDY INTO HER MOUTH, SEEMINGLY UNAWARE OF MY PRESENCE. THEN, SUDDENLY, HER EYES FLEW OPEN AND FIXED ON ME WITH AN EMPTY GAZE THAT SENT SHIVERS DOWN MY SPINE.

AS THE NIGHT GREW DARKER, THE ROOM'S SHADOWS SEEMED ALIVE. THE CLOUDS BEGAN TO SWIRL AND COALESCE UNTIL THEY FORMED A SOLID WALL OF DARKNESS THAT NO LIGHT COULD PENETRATE. THEN, SUDDENLY, A SHRILL SCREAM FILLED THE AIR, AND I KNEW SOMETHING SINISTER WAS LURKING BEYOND THE SWIRLING WALL OF DARKNESS.

SHE WAS WALKING AROUND HER NEW APARTMENT, ADMIRING THE PATTERN ON THE WALLS, WHEN SUDDENLY SHE NOTICED SOMETHING MOVE. SHE NERVOUSLY FOLLOWED IT, AND AS SHE PEERED AROUND THE CORNER, SHE SAW A FIGURE STANDING IN THE SHADOWS, STARING RIGHT BACK AT HER.

THE ROOM'S WALLS WERE FILLED WITH AN ARRAY OF BRIGHTLY COLORED SQUARES. THE COLORS STARTED SHIFTING AND MORPHING INTO SOMETHING SINISTER AS I STEPPED FORWARD. SUDDENLY, I FELT SOMETHING COLD AND SLIMY WRAP AROUND MY ARM WITH A FORCE THAT PULLED ME CLOSER TO THE WALL.

AS I WALKED THROUGH THE HALLWAY OF MY HOME, I NOTICED A SCORCHING FLOOR. I CAUTIOUSLY STEPPED TO THE SIDE AND PUT MY HAND DOWN TO FEEL IT, BUT IT FELT LIKE IT WAS BOILING. THEN, SUDDENLY, A LARGE HAND SEEMED TO GRAB ME FROM BENEATH THE FLOORBOARDS AND PULL ME DOWN INTO THE DARKNESS.

THE TEMPERATURE IN THE ROOM SUDDENLY DROPPED, AND THE WALLS BEGAN TO SWEAT. AS I LOOKED AROUND, I NOTICED THE WALLS WERE SLOWLY MELTING INTO ME. FINALLY, I REALIZED I WAS GETTING ABSORBED INTO THE WALLS AND COULD FEEL MY LIFE FADING AWAY.

THE COLD MARBLE FLOOR FELT LIKE ICE AGAINST MY BARE FEET AS I CREPT DOWN THE LONG, DARK HALLWAY. SHADOWS DANCED ALONG THE WALLS, SHIFTING AND WRITHING IN A SINISTER WAY THAT MADE MY HEART RACE. THEN, SUDDENLY, I HEARD A FAINT WHISPER FROM THE FLOOR BELOW ME, AND I KNEW SOMETHING WAS WRONG.

THE YOUNG GIRL WAS LYING IN BED WHEN SHE SUDDENLY NOTICED HER SKIN HAD STARTED TO CHANGE COLOR. IT WAS TURNING A DEEP, BRIGHT RED, LIKE THE BLOOD OF A FRESHLY SLAUGHTERED ANIMAL. SHE COULD FEEL THE HEAT RADIATING OFF HER BODY, AND THE MYSTERIOUS TRANSFORMATION FILLED HER WITH OVERWHELMING DREAD.

THE DARK, DAMP CAGE WALLS SEEMED TO CLOSE AROUND THEM, AND THEY KNEW THEY WOULD NEVER SEE THE LIGHT OF DAY IF THEY DIDN'T ESCAPE SOON. STRUGGLING AGAINST THE IRON BARS, THEY WERE DETERMINED TO BREAK FREE. THEN, JUST AS THEIR STRENGTH WAS WANING AND HOPE WAS FADING, A MYSTERIOUS FIGURE APPEARED FROM THE SHADOWS AND OFFERED THEM A WAY OUT.

THE YOUNG GIRL NERVOUSLY PUSHED ASIDE THE THICK COLORED CURTAINS. SHE GASPED IN HORROR AT WHAT SHE SAW BEHIND THEM; A PALE FIGURE WITH GLOWING EYES AND A SICKLY GRIN STOOD IN THE DARKNESS. THEN, SHE FELT AN ICY CHILL RUNNING DOWN HER SPINE AS SHE REALIZED THE FIGURE WAS STANDING RIGHT IN FRONT OF HER.

THE OLD LADY WAS ALWAYS HEARD IN THE DEAD OF NIGHT. SHE WOULD CALL OUT, HER VOICE ECHOING THROUGH THE DARK HALLWAYS OF THE ABANDONED MANSION. ONE NIGHT, A BRAVE SOUL DECIDED TO INVESTIGATE, ONLY TO DISCOVER THAT THE LADY HAD BEEN DEAD FOR YEARS.

THE SOUND OF SHATTERING GLASS WOKE ME FROM MY SLUMBER. I CAUTIOUSLY WALKED TOWARDS THE SOURCE OF THE SOUND, MY HEART POUNDING. AS I ROUNDED THE CORNER, I WAS MET WITH A GROTESQUE TABLEAU OF BROKEN GLASS WALLS AND MANGLED LIMBS.

THE SUN SHONE BRIGHTLY, ILLUMINATING THE SKY WITH A RAINBOW THAT SEEMED TO STRETCH ON FOREVER. AS I WALKED CLOSER, I REALIZED THAT THE SHIMMERING END OF THE RAINBOW WAS A PORTAL TO ANOTHER WORLD. I DISCOVERED A DARK AND TWISTED LAND FILLED WITH UNKNOWN HORRORS WHEN I STEPPED THROUGH.

AS THE SUN SET, A WOMAN MADE HER WAY TO THE INFAMOUS HOUSE OF ELEMENTS. LITTLE DID SHE KNOW, THE HOUSE WAS ALIVE WITH DARK AND SINISTER FORCES. TAKING ONE STEP INSIDE, SHE WAS IMMEDIATELY STRUCK WITH AN OVERWHELMING FEELING OF DREAD THAT CHILLED HER TO THE BONE.

THE GIRL'S BEDROOM WAS PAINTED A DEEP, EERIE SHADE OF PINK. SHE HAD NEVER FELT COM-
FORTABLE IN HER ROOM, BUT THE FEELING WAS COMPELLING. AS SHE LAY IN BED, SHE HEARD THE
FAINT SOUND OF SOMETHING SCRATCHING AT THE WALLS, AND SOON AFTER, SHE FELT THE OPPRES-
SIVE WEIGHT OF A PRESENCE RADIATING FROM THE PINK WALL OF PAIN.

WALKING DOWN THE ALLEYWAY, I COULD FEEL AN EERIE PRESENCE LOOMING ABOVE ME. WHEN I TURNED AROUND TO CONFRONT WHATEVER IT WAS, I SAW A FACE OF TERROR THAT SENT CHILLS DOWN MY SPINE. THEN, I KNEW THIS NIGHT WOULD BE ONE OF TERROR AND DREAD.

THE HOUSE WAS EERILY SILENT AS I STEPPED INSIDE. EVERYTHING SEEMED TO BE IN PLACE, YET SOMETHING FELT OFF. AS I WALKED THROUGH THE HALLWAY, I COULD FEEL THE WALLS TREMBLING, AS IF THEY WERE TRYING TO TELL ME SOMETHING BUT COULDN'T QUITE PUT IT TOGETHER.

THE NIGHT WAS QUIET, EXCEPT FOR THE WIND STIRRING THE COTTON CANDY WALL AT THE CARNIVAL. AS I WALKED CLOSER, I SAW A FIGURE SILHOUETTED AGAINST IT. BUT AS I REACHED OUT TO TOUCH IT, THE FIGURE LET OUT A PIERCING SCREAM AND VANISHED INTO THIN AIR. NOTHING REMAINED BUT A LINGERING SCENT OF SUGARY SWEETNESS, AND AN ICY CHILL RAN DOWN MY SPINE.

SHE HAD ALWAYS BEEN KNOWN FOR HER COLORFUL HAIR, BUT SOMETHING SEEMED TO CHANGE WHEN SHE RECENTLY DYED IT PURPLE. EVERYWHERE SHE WENT, PEOPLE WERE STARING AT HER. THEN ONE NIGHT, WHEN SHE AWOKE IN THE MIDDLE OF THE NIGHT, SHE LOOKED INTO THE MIRROR AND SAW THAT HER PURPLE HAIR WAS NOW A DEEP BLACK... AND IT SEEMED ALIVE.

SHE HAD BEEN ADMIRING THE NEW BLUE SUEDE SKIN IN THE STORE WINDOW ALL DAY AND DECIDED TO BUY IT. WHEN SHE TRIED IT ON, IT FELT STRANGELY ALIVE AGAINST HER BODY. LOOKING AT HERSELF IN THE MIRROR, SHE NOTICED STRANGE PURPLE VEINS FORMING ON HER SKIN AND REALIZED THAT THE BLUE SUEDE SKIN WAS SLOWLY TAKING OVER HER BODY.

THE CIRCUS HAD GONE STRANGELY SILENT AS THE CROWD FILED IN. THEN, AS THE SPOTLIGHT SHONE ON THE CLOWN, SOMETHING SEEMED OFF. HIS PAINTED SMILE WAS TOO BROAD, AND HIS MOVEMENTS TOO JERKY AS HE STUMBLED ACROSS THE STAGE, REVEALING A PAIR OF STUMPS WHERE HIS LEGS SHOULD HAVE BEEN.